MW01137645

Serving HIM

Vol. I

By Cassie Wild and M.S. Parker

Copyright © 2015 Belmonte Publishing
Published by Belmonte Publishing.

ISBN-13: 978-1512267877
ISBN-10: 1512267872:

Table of Contents

Chapter 1

Aleena

I'd be willing to bet if you asked a number of people my age what they planned to do on their twenty-first birthday, it would involve something along the lines of copious amounts of alcohol, and maybe a strip club. I know that was pretty close to what I'd had in mind.

I certainly hadn't counted on waiting tables during the lunchtime rush at one of New York's priciest restaurants. And yet, that's what I was doing.

Biting back a sigh, I shifted my weight as I wove through the sea of tables and flesh, carrying my burden of overpriced, oversized lunch entrees.

I'd come to New York City six months ago. Like so many others, I'd left my small-town life —Iowa for me— and come to the big city, but so far, nothing was turning out the way I'd hoped. Granted, it might have helped if I'd actually had some sort of plan in mind. Something other than *I'm tired of not fitting in, I'm tired of not belonging*.

Now, instead of not fitting in anywhere in small-town Iowa, I got to not fit in here in New York, one of the biggest cities in the world.

I'd hoped coming here would help me figure out who I was, what I wanted to do with my life. Since then, I'd figured out exactly one thing—I was a half-decent server. Nothing earth shattering. Nothing that steered me in a new direction.

I did learn one thing about myself—I preferred the city. I did miss my dad, even though I talked to him once a week. I sometimes felt guilty that I never got homesick, but there was little to miss about my old life. My mom had died when I was eight and my grandmother a few years ago. Now, other than my dad, there was nobody else left I really cared about.

"Here you go!" I smiled at the group of people gathered at table 216 and passed out the plates. Not a single one of them looked up, or spoke.

One of these days, I might get used to people totally ignoring me. Back home, people said *thank you* when you gave them something or at least offered a smile of appreciation.

Here? People acted like *they* did you a *favor* by *letting* you serve them.

That's just one of the differences between the

Midwest and the East Coast. Just one.

As they dug into their meals, I gathered up empties and stacked them on my tray. I was checking out the tables when I heard my name.

"Aleena!"

One of the other servers nudged me and I looked up to see my best friend, Molly, give me a quick wave from back near the kitchen. I grinned at her and gave a head bob in return, the best I could do with both of my hands full.

Molly Walters was three years older than me. With bright red hair, freckles and a wide, open smile, she'd been asked more than once if she was still in high school. The fact that she was tiny, the very definition of petite, didn't help any. She'd been working here for two years and had been the one to show me the ropes when I'd gotten hired. She wasn't just the closest person to me in the city. She was the closest friend I had, period.

She glanced around and then pointed at something she held.

I widened my eyes at the cupcake she held in one hand.

It was gone in the next instant, but I'd gotten a good look. It was one of those little ones with icing piled up so high on the top that it was almost bigger than the cake itself. Best of all, there was a candle right in the middle.

A blast of pleasure swam through me, almost obliterating this shit ass of a day. My feet were *killing* me. I'd been working for well over five hours and I didn't foresee a break in my near future. I wasn't even going to think about the three separate patrons who'd decided it was perfectly acceptable to cuss me out.

Oh, yeah. My asshole of a manager had 'accidentally' touched my ass twice this morning.

He'd asked me out my first day on the job. He'd been subtle about it and had seemed congenial when I told him no, but I could see the displeasure in his eyes.

Ever since, he'd gone out of his way to make my life pure hell here.

Molly kept saying I should file a lawsuit against him, but I didn't know what I was supposed to say.

He glared at me?

He glared at everybody.

He scowled a lot?

He wore a permanent scowl.

Every time he'd *accidentally* gotten too close, I could think of a dozen times when I'd legitimately accidentally bumped into somebody too. Accidents did sometimes happen.

Reporting him would cost me my job. People can talk all they want about *affirmative action* and *equal opportunity,* but if you were broke and barely scraping it by from day to day, sometimes, you were just...stuck. You had to have money to live, right?

Molly worked here with me—she'd helped me get the job. Any day with her made the day better. Thoughts of her and my birthday cupcake danced in my mind as I turned.

An older woman, walking with her friend, gesticulating wildly. "Can't you see how things are just going *south* in this country?" the woman demanded of her friend. As she spoke, she flung out an arm, catching me right in the face.

Pain flooded through me, a starburst from my cheekbone. I stumbled and the pain teleported to my ankle. I had a split second to register that my cheek hurt more than my ankle, but it didn't matter—I was going down. I was going to hit the floor and dishes were going to fly—

Then hands caught me and I stumbled into a hard body. The scent of a spicy cologne flooded my head.

Both appreciation and apprehension twined through me—appreciation for the as-yet-unseen male, and apprehension for the plates I couldn't hope to keep balanced.

"I got you," he said.

Yeah...you do, I thought, dazed.

For the briefest of moments, I thought he'd even catch the plates. They teetered on the brink before they crashed to the floor.

Silence descended. The odd kind that always follows such a spectacle spread throughout the restaurant. For that brief moment, I was able to just stand there. A body of solid, hard muscle held me steady. Through the thin back of my cotton dress-shirt, I felt the rise and fall of his chest. Carefully, I eased away and turned, lifting my head to gaze into a pair of the brightest blue eyes I'd ever seen.

My heart gave a hard thump.

Oh...wow.

He was almost too pretty. That hard jaw saved him from it, though it was close. His mouth curled as our eyes met and hot, sweet heat spread through me. He smiled and my heart fluttered just the slightest. There were disarming grooves that framed his mouth. A few years ago, they had probably been an amazing set of dimples and now, they made for a smile that probably threw women, young and old, off-guard.

"Hello."

"Thank you," I said.

Chatter resumed, people no longer interested.

Dishes had been broken, but nobody was hurt or angry—life will go on, right?

Or...maybe not.

A split second later, I heard the *clop-clop-clop* of thick-soled shoes. Dread twisted in me and I looked up in time to see a short, stocky man striding toward me.

My boss.

The scowling ass-grabber.

Gary was in his mid-thirties, but dressed and acted ten years older. His hair was already thinning, but instead of accepting his losses and cutting it short, he left it long and combed it back, slicking it with some sort of hair grease that smelled like coconuts.

He often reminded me of a rodent—his complexion ruddy even on the best of days. Today wasn't the best of days. He was red, so red it would have worried me if I hadn't seen my fate dancing before me.

Some of the people close to us cast curious glances our ways. Nervous, I smoothed down my skirt. I *hated* being the center of attention.

As he drew nearer, I couldn't decide if I'd rather have him do this here or back in his office. I never liked being alone with Gary, but I thought it might be worth it just so I didn't have all these people staring at me, including the extremely hot man standing so close I could still smell his cologne or whatever it was he was wearing.

"Come with me." Gary grabbed me, his fat fingers digging into the flesh of my upper arm.

Shame made my skin grow hot and I focused on

7

the floor as we passed by the patrons. I could hear his murmured apologies. *"I'm so sorry. Please excuse this inconvenience..."*

This wasn't going to end well.

The moment the door shut behind us, I twisted free.

"What the hell were you doing? Don't you know how to carry plates?"

I guess there wasn't a point in telling him that somebody had hit me. My cheek still stung from the blow. Swallowing, I just stared at him.

"You made a fucking mess out there!" He stabbed a finger toward the door. "What sort of incompetent idiot *are* you?"

I could ask you the same thing, I thought mutinously. My dad ran the best restaurant back in our hometown and one thing he'd drilled into my head—*you treat your staff the way you'd want to be treated. You treat them with respect and they'll respect you.*

But Gary didn't want my respect.

He wanted in my pants.

So I just stared at him. It only made him angrier.

He opened his mouth. Dread curdled in my gut.

Aw, no.

I needed this job.

"I don't even know why I let Molly talk me into hiring you."

You hired me because you wanted to get into my pants. I had to bite my tongue to keep from saying it. Erring on the side of diplomacy, I said, "I'm really sorry, Gary. It won't happen again."

"I know it won't." He crossed his arms over his chest.

No, no, no...

Just then, the door opened and the hot guy who'd caught me walked in as if he owned the place.

"Gary, right?" He flashed a charming smile.

Gary gaped at him for a split second and then shook himself, attempting to regain his composure. "Sir, you can't be in here."

"I just wanted to help straighten things out." He glanced at me and then nodded at Gary. "You see, Gary, what happened out there wasn't her fault."

I wasn't sure who was more surprised, Gary or me.

"It was mine."

He took a step forward and I suddenly realized how big he was. In the rush of the moment earlier, I'd missed it, but he was almost a foot taller than me—and so damn sexy. He wore a suit that fit him so well, I didn't doubt it had been specially made for him.

"I didn't look where I was going and I bumped into her." He reached into his back pocket and pulled out his wallet. "Let me pay for the damages."

9

"Sir, that's really not necessary," Gary said. A smile now crossed his face, replacing the snarl. It held a world of ass-kissing in it. *Have money? Will grovel.*

"Nonsense. I insist." He held out a couple hundred dollars. "And I'm sure whatever else is left over, you can find some use for." He smiled at Gary, but his eyes flicked over to me. "No one needs to get fired, right?"

"Of course not, sir." Gary took the money and gave a slow nod. "I appreciate your kindness and understanding."

The knight-gallant gave Gary a pointed look. "I'd like a word with the young lady, please."

"Oh, of course." Gary hurried out without a second glance at me.

I waited until the door closed before looking up at the man who'd just saved my job. "Thank you so much."

"You're very welcome." He smiled at me, this one much more genuine than the ones he'd given Gary. He glanced back at the door my manager had disappeared through. "It wasn't your fault. The lady...she caught you in the face pretty hard."

"I'm fine," I said, smiling. I lifted my hand to my sore cheek.

"Are you?"

"I..." I swallowed.

10

He glanced at the door again and then looked back at me. "Are you?"

"I'm fine," I repeated, although I wasn't entirely sure it was true. Our eyes met and there was a moment of silence before I felt compelled to break it. "I should get going. My shift's not over until four."

"Be careful," he said. "I'm leaving so I won't be here to catch you if you have another accident."

As he spoke, he reached out to touch my arm— that light contact sent heat blazing up through me. My breath caught in my throat. Heat pooled down low in my belly and to my horror, I could feel my nipples drawing tight, stabbing into my bra.

Oooookay.

I needed to get out of here before I made a bigger fool of myself than I already had. He left first, though, quickly and quietly, out the door before I had a chance.

I gave myself thirty seconds. Thirty seconds to calm myself and then I slid out of Gary's office and headed to the kitchen. Hopefully somebody had been watching my orders.

"What the hell are you still doing here?" Gary snapped.

I came up short. "Ah...I still have a couple hours left on my shift."

Gary scowled at me and I knew.

"You said you wouldn't fire me." I took a couple

11

steps forward, lowering my voice. My stomach churned.

He smiled at me, but it was a cold one, one that turned my stomach. "Let me give you a piece of advice that will help you for the rest of your life."

"Yeah?" I stared at him, jerking my chin up. I was tired of him talking down to me. If he was going to fire me anyway—and I had a feeling he was—then I was done trying to play nice.

"You know that saying that the customer's always right?"

"What about it?" I asked.

"Well, it's bullshit." Gary jerked his head toward the office. "And that was the perfect example. Go get your stuff. Leave and don't come back."

"You son of a bitch," I said, months of suppressed anger and humiliation breaking free. I reached up to touch my necklace, telling myself to calm down. It wasn't that bad. It was never that bad, right?

But my necklace was gone.

"What did you say to me?" Gary's eyes flew wide.

Ignoring him, I patted at my neck. "My necklace..."

"Get out!" Gary shouted.

I looked around, staring at the floor, searching for the silver chain.

"Didn't you hear me?!"

"I can't find my necklace!" I shouted back at him.

"I don't care about your necklace," Gary snapped, storming over and grabbing my arm. His fingers dug into my skin, drawing a pained yelp out of me. "Get the hell out or I'll call someone to get you out."

He shook me and then, with a final squeeze, shoved me toward the door. "Get out."

Tears of anger and misery spilled over.

I didn't want him to see, so I turned away.

Earlier, I'd thought how odd it was that I hadn't been homesick.

Swallowing the knot in my throat, I half-stumbled toward the door.

Suddenly, I was very, very homesick.

Chapter 2

Aleena

"Honey, I can't find it."

I squeezed my eyes shut. "You looked? Everywhere?"

"Yeah. I looked."

Fisting a hand in my hair, I pressed the back of my skull against the wall. "Maybe I should come in and check. It could—"

"Don't." Molly said quickly, her voice somber. "Gary has already told people that if you show up, they're to call the cops. Anybody who doesn't might lose their job. I'll keep a look out for it, okay?"

I sniffed and wiped at the tears that seemed to chase me all day.

"Okay."

I hung up the phone and retreated to my narrow bed. I couldn't call it a room. If you wanted private space in Manhattan, you better find a job that paid a lot more than you could make on a server's salary. I had a roommate and while we were lucky enough to have room for two people, we didn't have room enough for two *bedrooms*.

I'd been surprised when I moved here.

The apartment I now shared with another person could have fit in the living room of the house where I grew up. People who haven't been in New York City don't get it. An apartment with eight hundred square feet is actually considered pretty roomy—and they can be horribly expensive.

I laid on my bed, staring out the window at the miserable view of the alley and thought about the view I'd had back home.

Did I miss it?

I didn't want to think I did.

Back home, nobody had ever yelled at me because I'd dropped a tray of plates.

But then again, back home, I was just as invisible as I was here.

Invisible.

Unnecessary.

I sighed and curled into my pillow. I didn't fit in here anymore than I had there.

No...this wasn't how I'd imagined spending my twenty-first birthday. I never even got to enjoy my cupcake.

I spent the night sulking.

If you lose your job, especially on your birthday, I figure you're entitled.

But the first thing I did the next day was get up and shower. I had to find a new job.

Friday was spent walking around, searching for employment. I had a couple of on-the-spot interviews and a couple of places took my number. One thing about New York, there is almost always a place looking for a girl—or guy—who can take orders. The problem is those jobs are taken almost as fast as they come up.

By the time I got back to my apartment, my feet were aching and I was freezing.

One of the interviews would pan out. I was almost certain of it.

Of course, I could end up in a job even worse than what I'd just lost. That was a thought that depressed me thoroughly. Maybe I'd been spoiled, working for my dad from the time I'd turned sixteen. Dad had taken over the Main Street Café from Grandma after she'd had a stroke. That was one of the reasons we'd moved there. That...and the fact that he'd wanted me to grow up with some sort of family around me.

Mom had died—breast cancer—and he was raising me by himself, working more than forty hours a week. I hardly ever saw him.

Then Grandma had the stroke.

We'd moved back to the small town where he'd grown up and for a short while, I'd been...almost happy. Grandma had recovered and moved back home and we'd all lived in the big old house where Dad had grown up. He took over at the restaurant and Grandma had been there when I got home from school and she'd been there on the weekends, even when Dad was working. When I'd started working at their restaurant, people had smiled and acted happy to see me.

There, more than anyplace else, I'd fit in.

It's terrible when the place you fit in more than anywhere else is a restaurant. Even worse when it's not even *your* restaurant...but the place your dad owns.

That's why I'd decided to leave. I'd wanted something else. Something more.

No.

Something *mine*.

All I'd ever wanted was someplace that was mine, something, anything that was mine.

Ducking into the bathroom, I pressed my back to the door. I was still cold, frozen to the bone and getting more depressed by the minute.

The bathroom of the small apartment was cramped, but its one redemptive quality was that it had a tub. A real tub, not just a stall for a shower. I got the hot water going and started to strip. The mirror reflected my image back at me and out of habit, I tried not to look.

But for some reason, I stopped.

Slowly, I straightened. My clothes fell from numb hands.

Staring at my reflection, I tried to see what others saw, what it was that seemed to be so...unappealing to others.

I'd come to grips with who I was—or at least, I thought I had.

My dad had been the town's golden boy, or that was the story I'd always heard. The Main Street Café was just part of the Davison legacy. My dad had been the quarterback on the football team. His dad had been the chief of police. His dad had been the mayor. *His* dad had been one of the town's few judges. They'd all been golden... or so it seemed.

Golden.

And unhappy.

Right up until my dad.

He'd been engaged to the daughter of the mayor. But he'd loved my mother.

My mom—a poor black girl who hadn't really had much chance at anything beyond working as a server at the Main Street Café—the same restaurant where she'd met my dad.

They'd run away together, two weeks before the wedding, and a year later I was born.

It's been over two decades now and not once in my life had I felt like I'd fit in.

I don't hate the girl I see in the mirror, but to be honest, I still don't know her.

Absently, I reached up and brushed my fingers across my cheek.

I had my mother's face, high cheekbones and heart-shaped face, my skin a warm smooth gold. My hair was curly and soft; my eyes were my father's, pale and light green.

I wasn't unattractive.

Logically, I knew that.

It wasn't even being biracial that made me such a misfit. I wasn't the only mixed kid back home. There were a few others. I was just the only one who didn't fit in.

But I'd never known how to do that anywhere.

Could I go back there?

Should I go back?

I brooded over that throughout my bath and was still debating when I retreated to bed. My roommate came in and I feigned sleep. I wasn't that tired yet, but I didn't want to talk either.

Emma could be a pain, but we had unspoken

rules—if the other was sleeping, we let the person be.

I couldn't avoid her forever, though. I owed her rent and I had to come up with the money soon.

I'd cut it close before, but I'd never been late until now. Tears burned my eyes and I pressed my face into my pillow to keep from making a sound. It took forever for me to fall into a restless sleep.

***

Morning came too early, too fast and too bright.

As quiet as possible, I rose from my bed and crept into the miniscule little alcove that served as a kitchen. There were no *real* rooms in our apartment, save for the bathroom so it was a futile attempt, but I tried.

I hadn't even managed to open a single cabinet before I heard her behind me.

"You're avoiding me."

I turned towards her. Emma Kane was twenty-five and gorgeous. Long, straight, white blond hair that never had a strand out of place. Hazel eyes and high cheekbones. She was nearly six feet tall and rail-thin. I hadn't been surprised when she'd told me she'd come to New York from Wisconsin to be a model. That had been eight years ago.

"No, Emma," I said wearily. "I was out looking

for a job yesterday. I ended up taking a bath and collapsing pretty much as soon as I finished. I was just...tired."

"Why were you looking for a job?" She angled her head to the side, studying me.

Shit. I'd forgotten to tell her. "One of the customers practically knocked me down. I dropped some plates. Gary fired me."

A good roommate would've gone on about how shitty that was and how my manager had been out of line. Not Emma.

"Does this mean you don't have your part of the rent?"

"Not yet." I grabbed a tea bag and shoved it into a cup of water. I was craving a cappuccino, but I couldn't afford it. I had to have some caffeine, though. So tea it was. "But I'll get it to you. I promise."

She scowled at me, crossing her arms. "I can't afford to carry your rent too, Aleena. That's why I needed a roommate in the first place."

"I know, Emma." Unable to look at her, I dug a bagel out of the freezer and popped it into the toaster. "I'm going out as soon as I'm done eating and I already had a couple of interviews yesterday. Something will come up soon."

Emma snorted, the sound clearly derisive. I fought the urge to flip her off.

Fortunately, she decided to remove temptation, spinning on her heel and striding away.

I had a few minutes of silence to eat my breakfast and then I headed outside.

January in New York is nasty but at least it was dry. As long as it was over zero and there wasn't any snow on the ground, I'd walk and save whatever money I could. After six months, I was almost used to not having a car.

Almost. But not quite.

By the time noon rolled around, I'd talked with yet another half dozen restaurants. I wanted to think something would happen, but I just didn't know.

Something would open up. I had to believe that. In a city the size of New York, with *how* many restaurants? There would be a thousand places, or more, in any given direction. Someplace had to need help.

It was close to one when I stopped in a small coffee shop and bought myself the cheapest, smallest drink I could. It was more to warm up than anything else. I didn't buy something to eat, although my stomach growled in protest.

I took a few more minutes and then hit the other direction.

Two of the spots I hit actually *did* show some promise, although one of them was so far away, I'd spend nearly forty minutes traveling there and back each day. Not exactly ideal. But beggars can't be choosers, right?

I had several business cards and a couple of promises for second interviews.

I'd hold on to that, I told myself. It wasn't much, but it was more than I'd had yesterday. Well, no. Not exactly. Yesterday, I had a job. A lousy one, but a job. But these were interviews, and neither of them had been at lousy places.

Trying to console myself with that, I headed back to the apartment. I was almost as exhausted now as I'd been last night when I finally went to bed. I couldn't imagine doing this again tomorrow.

So don't.

I almost brushed the idea aside and then I stopped.

Well, maybe I shouldn't. Tomorrow was Sunday. Emma was off. She always spent her day off with her guy, Malachi. I'd have some peace and quiet while I checked some things out online.

***

Sunday was a bust.

Monday promised to be the same—one of my supposed-second interviews called me to reschedule and another cancelled outright.

Molly called a little before noon. "Are you busy?" She didn't even bother with a greeting.

I sighed. "Yes, but I'd prefer not to be. I've been out since eight looking for work."

"You need lunch," Molly said. In her opinion, food made everything a little bit better. "Where are you?"

I squinted and then answered. "Not too far from MoMa."

The Museum of Modern Art and the area around it was normally one of my favorite areas, but I wasn't there to hang out or kill time. I was job hunting—still—and not having much luck with it either.

"Awesome. Listen, there's this place..." She gave me an address. "Meet me there in thirty, okay?"

The café Molly sent me to was small and out of the way. It was the sort of kitschy place I'd love to work, but when I asked if they were hiring, the lady gave me a polite smile and shook her head. She did give me an application to fill out. I did—you never know, right?

I was busy working on it when Molly arrived. She dropped into the seat across from me and smiled. I smiled back, but my heart wasn't really in it.

"How are you?" she asked, concern softening her voice.

"I've been better," I said. I looked up as the

25

waiter came towards us, mentally counting the change I had in my pockets.

"I've got this," Molly said. Before I could argue, the waiter was there and Molly was ordering two cups of coffee. When he walked away, she turned back to me. "I worked a double yesterday, so I've got some extra tip money."

I scowled. "So I haven't been replaced yet?"

"No." She grimaced. "Gary's an asshole, you know that?"

I didn't want to ask, because I was pretty sure I already knew the answer. Even if I was wrong, I was even more certain I didn't want to do it. Still, I was desperate. "Is there any chance I could get my job back? They haven't replaced me and I wouldn't need training."

Molly's expression told me the answer before she said it. "Again, Gary's an asshole."

Scowling, I folded my arms across my chest and slumped in my seat. "You know, he's just pissed off at me because I wouldn't go out with him."

"Yeah." Molly looked away. "Most of the people there know it. But most of the people, me included, kind of need their jobs."

"Hey..." I reached out and touched her arm. "I don't blame you. I get it, really."

"Thanks." She gave me a sad smile. Then, jerking her shoulder in a shrug, she said, "If he wasn't the owner's nephew, he would've been out on his ass years ago. But I didn't ask you here to talk about that loser. Let's talk about something fun."

Rolling my eyes, I said, "Then you better drive the conversation. I don't have anything fun to talk about."

"Okay." Molly wagged her eyebrows at me. "I do. I slept with Delphine last night."

"What?!" I gaped at her.

And just like that, we were off. Molly kept up the conversation after her play-by-play of her night with Delphine, the hot junior chef Molly had been eyeing for weeks. Normally, her transitioning into my own lack of a love life would've annoyed me, but this time, even that was a welcome distraction.

As Molly set some cash down on the table, her face suddenly lit up.

"I almost forgot!" She dug through her purse for several seconds before emerging with a small, rectangular card.

She held it out to me. "A guy came by the restaurant and gave me his number for you. He said he found your necklace."

"And you're just telling me this now?!" I snatched the card from her, blinking back the tears that suddenly burned my eyes. "He found my grandmother's necklace."

"Sorry." She grinned at me and gave me a

lascivious wink. Molly made no secret of the fact she was bisexual. In so many ways, Molly was my mirror opposite. "He was hot too. I was tempted to ask if I could come by and get the necklace for you."

I gave her an absent smile as I stared at the card. Dominic Snow. There wasn't anything else on the card to explain who Dominic Snow was, but I didn't care. He had my grandmother's necklace. I'd given up ever seeing it again. It took all of my self-control not to ignore Molly and call the number right now.

At least *one* thing didn't totally suck right now.

Either Molly sensed my impatience or she was ready to go because she didn't linger over good-byes like she usually did. Instead, she just got up and gave me a hug before she headed out.

I decided to stay a bit longer so I could make my call without the noise of the city's chaos. I still needed to cover a few more places before I went home and I didn't want to wait that long to call.

"Hello?" The man's voice was pleasant and vaguely familiar. That didn't mean anything though. In the six months I'd been waiting tables, I'd talked to thousands of men. He could've been any of them.

"Hi, this is Aleena Davison." I paused, then realized that he might not know my name. "You have my necklace."

"Ah, yes, Aleena." He sounded...what was it? I couldn't quite put my finger on it. Amused? Pleased?

Frowning, I concentrated on his words instead of that odd tone. And the sexiness of it.

"I was hoping you'd call," he continued. "This piece of jewelry appears to be fairly old and I assumed it was something quite special."

"It is," I said. Suddenly, I was nervous, wondering if I should have stayed silent. Now that he knew it was important, he might think that he could get some money out of me.

"Unfortunately, I'm out of town on a business trip at the moment," he said. "But I'll be back in the morning. Can you meet me?"

"Um, sure." I waited for it, the price-tag.

"Do you know Bouley?"

I silently swore. Bouley was a hot-spot for the high-spending execs—the kind of money I *did not* have. They've got five-course lunches, well-priced, I guess, if you can afford to spend money on a *five-course* lunch in a *five-star* restaurant.

I can't even afford a soda there.

"Yes, I know it." I was also pretty sure I didn't own anything I could wear to it. I couldn't tell if he'd just invited me to have a drink, but I certainly wasn't about to show up looking like I worked there.

"Would you be able to meet me there tomorrow at noon?"

What could I say to that? I wanted—no, I needed—my grandmother's necklace back. So I'd look like a loser and just order ice water.

"Sure."

"Great. I'll see you then."

And just like that I was going to meet a complete stranger at a fancy restaurant.

Chapter 3

Aleena

Bouley was just as nice inside as it was out. I smoothed down the sweater-dress I'd borrowed from Emma.

I say *borrow* although technically it was more like I swiped it out of her closet after she left for work. I'd already planned to take care of her laundry tonight to make up for not getting the rent money to her. I'd just add the dress to it.

Considering the difference in our body types, the dress actually fit pretty well. I figured my curves stretched it enough to compensate for the height difference. The color had been the deciding factor. It was a rich, deep red, the kind that looked good on true blonds like Emma or on those with a darker complexion like me.

"Are you meeting someone?" The hostess smiled at me as I came inside.

"Dominic Snow." I gave her the name he'd said on the phone.

"Right this way."

I followed her, trying not to fidget with the dress or my hair. All those thoughts fled when I saw who was sitting at the table.

My mouth went dry.

My hands went clammy.

Shit.

The hot stranger from the other day, the one who'd stopped me from falling and had tried to save my job, he was Dominic Snow. He was the guy who had my necklace. And judging by the lack of surprise on his face, he'd known who I was.

"You don't seem surprised to see me," I said as he stood and pulled out my chair.

"I'm not." He flashed me that same charming smile. "I found the necklace on the floor near the plates when I went back to my table to get my jacket. I wasn't positive it belonged to you, but I suspected as much."

Is he flirting with me? I didn't know. I'd never been as good at reading these signals as some girls.

"I know I asked you to meet me here so I could give you the necklace, but my business meeting just canceled on me. Would you care to join me? My treat, of course." He settled back down in his seat and reached for his water glass. "I do hate to eat alone."

Get the necklace. Get out. Common sense told me that was the smart thing to do.

And my stomach chose that moment to growl.

Hunger won out over common sense. I hadn't had a decent meal in two days—my groceries were all but gone and it wasn't like I had money coming in tomorrow, right?

"I'd like that, thank you."

He smiled at me and gestured a server over. "Would you like some wine?"

"No, thanks." I smiled as I answered.

He nodded and ordered a glass for himself.

I asked for water. We chatted about the food while we went over the menu. We had barely closed the menus before the server arrived to take our orders.

Once that was done, he leaned back in his chair and those extraordinary blue eyes focused on me.

"So, Miss Aleena Davison...it is Miss, right?" His smile flashed, hot and bright, and his eyes glinted at me.

"Yes." I held up my left hand and wiggled my fingers. Then, surprising myself with my boldness, I raised an eyebrow and gave his hand a pointed look.

"Yes," he said as he held up his hand. "I'm a Miss too."

I laughed, and he immediately joined in, a low

rumbling sound that made heat coil in my stomach.

As that tug of heat spread, I reached for my water. I'd hoped the reaction I'd felt the other day had been a fluke.

"You're not from around here, are you?" He took a sip of his wine. "No accent."

I shook my head. "I'm from Iowa. And you?"

"Me?" There was a flicker of surprise in his eyes, gone so fast I barely had a chance to recognize it.

"You don't have an accent either," I pointed out.

"True. But I'm New York, born and raised." He lifted a brow, a faint smile curling his lips. "In the business world, especially when dealing internationally, it's...better to have a more general American accent."

As we talked, I began to relax. It was nice, sitting in a good restaurant, eating the kind of food I couldn't afford on my own. He was attractive—*whoa* he was extremely attractive and that laugh. Every time it rolled through the room, I felt a tug deep inside me.

Not that he was flirting, exactly.

Occasionally, his eyes would linger on mine, but there was nothing less than courtesy in the way he acted and after the way my past few days had gone, it was something I desperately needed.

Since this was the first—and probably the last—time I'd had the chance to sit down in a high dollar restaurant with an urbane guy like Dominic, I planned to enjoy it.

Enjoy wasn't the right word, though.

He wasn't just sexy, and there was more to him than that amazing smile. He made me laugh. He had an insightful way of looking at things and a kind way of treating others. He gave the server who brought our food the same courtesy he'd shown me—and that meant something.

Since it was the same job I had, it mattered to me when a guy didn't treat others in that line of work as invisible.

Before I knew it, our plates were being cleared and the server was asking about dessert. Regret was something I was familiar with, but I can't ever recall feeling it quite as strongly as I did then.

"Thank you, no," Dominic said after I'd declined.

As the server walked away, Dominic looked at me. He reached into his coat pocket. "I should probably give you this."

The chain of my grandmother's necklace glinted in the subtle lighting overhead. "Wouldn't want to forget the reason you came."

My heart leaped at the sight of it and then it practically stopped when our fingers brushed. As a gasp lodged in my throat, I looked up at him. He was watching me, his gaze intent on mine.

"Thank you," I said, my throat almost painfully dry. As he continued to stare at me, something unfamiliar settled inside me. I curled the chain in my palm and tucked both hands in my lap. "Thank you so much. My grandmother gave it to me before she passed."

"You were close?" he murmured. "It hurts to lose somebody you love. I'm sorry."

"Yes." I looked away. There really wasn't anything else to say, was there?

"We should go," he said a moment later. "I hope I'm not making you late for work or anything. Wouldn't want to give your boss another reason to bother you." His mouth tightened.

"Ah...not likely." I placed my napkin on the table, taking care not to look at him. "I don't currently *have* a boss."

It's amazing how much tension can flood a silence. It startled me enough that I looked over at him. His jaw was tight, almost rigid with anger, but the moment our eyes met, the expression was gone.

"I see." He drummed his fingers on the table. "Are you job hunting then?"

"Yes." I gave him my best, *everything's fine* smile. I had a lot of practice with it. I could bluster with the best of them. I'd been doing it most of my life.

He looked thoughtful for a moment and then he

leaned forward. "What sort of jobs have you done?" he asked.

"Excuse me?"

"Humor me." He gave me that quick smile again, those grooves beside his mouth deepening. That smile could probably be classified as a deadly weapon.

Uncertain where he was going with this, I shrugged. "I've been serving since I was sixteen. It's what I'm best at. But I took office administration in college and was one of the assistant managers at my dad's restaurant from the time I was eighteen up until I decided to move here. I can do office work— Microsoft Word, Excel, that sort of thing. I helped out with payroll until I finally convinced Dad he'd be better off switching to a service."

"So you're organized."

"Guilty." I gave him a look of mock sincerity.

He didn't smile. Instead, he went back to tapping one finger on the table. Just one—his index finger. After a moment, he stopped and then leaned back into his seat. "I know of a company that's having open interviews tomorrow for several different jobs. I can't guarantee anything, but I can't see them not being able to find a place for you."

What? I had to struggle not to gape at him.

"Here." He took out a business card and a pen, and scribbled something on the back. "Here's the address. The interviews start at eight."

I took the card and lifted it up, staring at it dumbly.

He rose and I shifted my gaze to look up at him.

He bent over it, gently pressing his lips against the back of my hand. "I hope to see you again."

I stared as he walked away, my heart racing and my mind half-dulled by the shock.

I could still feel the place on my hand where his mouth had been.

I hoped he'd see me again too.

Chapter 4

Dominic

Don't look back, I told myself.

She was...intriguing.

She was sexy as hell, but I knew plenty of attractive women. I'd noticed her even before that disaster in the restaurant. Who *wouldn't* notice her? Her hair, her eyes—that ass?

But I knew any number of beautiful women.

There was still a bruise on her cheek from where she'd inadvertently been hit. It infuriated me to see a bruise on a woman, but it wasn't like it had been done out of cruelty. Carelessness yes, but cruelty, no.

It was the bruises in her eyes that were really twisting me up.

That dick of a manager.

As I climbed into my car, I gave my driver an absent greeting, but my mind wasn't on him or even on the rest of the days' business. But her.

I'd tried to diffuse the situation between her and

the dick, but it hadn't worked.

It hadn't been her fault, but you couldn't tell it by the way that asshole had acted.

I'd left there feeling like a hero. Now I felt like a heel. It wasn't a feeling I cared for.

"Will you require your usual pick-up, Mr. Snow?"

The driver's question cut through my thoughts and I looked around, realizing we were already at my office.

"Six o'clock," I said. "I'm thinking dinner and then heading out to a club."

"Very good, sir."

Sighing, I said, "*Dominic*, Mike."

"Yes, sir." A faint smile flashed across his face.

I shook my head as he stopped at the curb and opened the door before he could get out to do it himself. He'd been my driver for four years and he still wouldn't call me anything but *Mr. Snow* or *sir*.

For a moment, I stood there, staring up at the jet-black spire that housed *Trouver L'Amour*.

What an irony.

Or maybe not. I believed in love—for others. I just didn't see it in the cards for myself. All the more reason not to think about a certain gorgeous, green-eyed sweetheart who was clearly cut out for forevers.

It was ironic, I thought, standing there in front of the office of *Trouver L'Amour*. It was marketed—

and indeed built—for the rich, jet-setting crowd, where we promised to help you find the ideal match for you.

I helped people find a forever of their own, but it was something that just wasn't in the cards for me.

Love just wasn't going to happen.

It was an emotion that had been all but destroyed...years ago.

Before the darkness of those memories could swim through and overtake me, I started inside.

The interior decorator who handled my other businesses was scheduled to come in tomorrow and we were going to be officially opening the first week in February. The open house on Valentine's Day would mark my official foray into the business of match making.

Winding through the workers who were busily getting everything into place, I found my office and settled in. My own work area was still relatively bare, just the essentials for now. The other furnishings would be brought in by Annette Shale, one of New York City's top designers. I didn't mind working like this. The excess wasn't for me, anyway. It was for the clients. Apparently, whether I preferred Van Gogh over some no-name artist meant I was better equipped to find them their ideal mate.

Not that I would be the one matching people up.

It wasn't all going to be done on a computer, either. We were promising a human touch. None of the clients needed to know that the detailed interview would be plugged into a computer, taking into account the myriad personality types. Those details would be combined with all the factors a real human being was needed for. It was the best of both worlds. The computer's efficiency, the human's empathy and intuition.

Tomorrow's open house was also looking for matchmakers.

While Aleena didn't have the qualifications for that, I wondered if there was something else here she might qualify for, but even as I considered it, I frowned.

She was sweet and kind, but she exuded an innocence and naiveté that would have too many people flocking to her like sharks scenting blood in the water.

Oh, not all of my clients were like that, but too many of them were. No matter how she dressed, no matter what she did or said, she would stand out.

I'd contact those handling the hiring and put her down as a top placement, but she wasn't to be put here.

Even as I made the decision, though, disappointment welled inside me.

Trouver L'Amour was just getting started and

for the next many months, this was where I'd be spending most of my time and energy.

No matter where she was sent, it'd be one of the family businesses, but I probably wouldn't see her again.

Don't think about it, Snow.

It wasn't like we were friends. Wasn't like we had anything in common. Wasn't like—

"Focus, Snow," I muttered. Shaking my head, I powered up my computer and went to the interview list my business manager had sent me. Robson Findlay had already noted a few names. I added Aleena's name and sent the email to him, adding in a quick note about her and the background she'd given me.

I never made promises about employment, but I never turned anyone away for an interview either. If she had the qualifications and there was an opening that would fit her, Rob would find her a job.

That task done, I settled down to deal with business, going over the plan I'd developed with a friend—also in the matchmaking industry.

But I wasn't able to focus.

I found myself thinking about the lush curve of her mouth.

Her ass.

The sweet, open innocence of her smile.

"Innocence," I said, shoving back from the desk

after I found myself distracted by her for the second time in an hour. Restless, edgy energy burned in me. It was the sort of tension I was too familiar with and under normal circumstances, I could have caged it and just waited until evening.

I didn't know if it was going to work though.

My mind was too full of her.

That innocent smile.

Those beautiful eyes.

Aleena was a sweet girl and that was the entire problem.

Sweet wasn't for me.

Sweet girls tended to expect things—and they were entirely right to do that.

I couldn't offer anything more than a night of hard, fast sex.

Besides, I was a businessman and I had to focus on the face of *Trouver L'Amour*. Any woman I dated needed to help drive the image of my company. It was shallow and I knew it. But it was how business worked.

When it came to sex, I had a different sort of woman in mind and Aleena didn't fit that, either.

Although...I swore and spun around, driving my fist into the hard, clear surface of the window. Now I had the image of her spread out on my bed, bound and open and ready for me, that innocent curiosity shining from her eyes. It was a picture that brought my cock to full, aching awareness.

It was an erotic thing to imagine, driving her to the brink, having her beg—my hand on her ass, bringing a blush to that golden flesh, hearing my name on her lips, knowing that her pleasure lay in my hands.

And it was about as likely as the sun rising in the west.

I took women to my bed who knew the score—they wanted sex and I wanted their submission.

That wasn't Aleena.

Miserable and aching, I leaned against the window.

Maybe I should have just given that necklace to her friend.

***

The sun was sinking below the horizon by the time Mikhail dropped me off at the private club I'd chosen for the night. I sent him on home. The club offered a car service for their VIP members.

A cold wind cut through me as I strode inside. The man at the door had it open, giving me a polite nod. Most people were ID'd as they went through, but most of the VIPS were recognized on sight.

Going from the still-brilliant light of day to the

club's dim exterior, I blinked, giving my eyes a moment to adjust.

The VIP section was in the back and I took my time taking the winding staircase that offered direct access. The area was elevated, offering a clear view of the rest of the area.

I walked along the upper level, not even registering the extremes that came with being a part of this world. While I personally never got into the wardrobe aspect that many others in this lifestyle gravitated towards, I'd seen them often enough that they didn't have much effect on me. Not that everyone here was dressed in leather and chains. One of the things I liked about Olympus was that it had a little bit of everything.

Within a few feet, I saw a female dominant leading her sub by a collar. The only thing he wore other than his collar was a cock ring. They walked past a trio of people in regular clubbing clothes— sexy, but nothing that screamed of the BDSM lifestyle. Two men behind them were dressed as I was, wearing well-cut, tailored suits.

Since it was the middle of the week, and still fairly early, the club wasn't as packed as usual. I saw only a few people I knew, but it didn't matter.

I wasn't looking to meet anybody.

Not tonight.

Only a few others were seated in the VIP section.

They sat in shadowed, dark areas, far enough away to make it clear they were in the mood for privacy.

That was good. I wasn't in the mood to converse with others about shared interests. I was feeling far too introspective for that. I settled in a similar seat and focused my attention on the stage, hoping that tonight's show would get my mind off of things.

One of the club's usual players was taking the stage. She called herself Mistress Rose, though I'd begun to suspect she was actually Patty Reimbaum, the personal secretary to the Manhattan DA. She wore a mask that covered most of her face and her light brown hair was always pulled back so it was impossible to tell the style or length.

She was beautiful. Her figure was exquisite, her body taut and toned, displayed in what most people would associated with a dominatrix. In one hand, she held a flogger.

The submissive who came on stage with her was young. I didn't recognize him. He didn't wear a mask. I hadn't been here in a while, so he might not be as new as he seemed. He was fit—that was pretty much par for the course in this place—and his body was bare save for a few piercings.

Mistress Rose wasn't one to waste time or mince words. As the music started to pulse, she led her sub to the X in the middle of the stage and tied him, making a production of it. Her hands glided over him and when she paused to stroke, anybody could see the anticipation that had his body already going to taut.

Others in the crowd watched with varying levels of appreciation.

I wasn't one of them.

I was...bored.

She was an artist at what she did, but she was predictable. Nothing she ever did was different, save for her clothing and her choice in subs. She broke him almost to the very brink, listened with a smile as he begged and from time to time, she'd pause and smile out over the crowd.

Are you enjoying yourself, she seemed to ask.

No. I wasn't. Aggravated, I looked away and stared out into the crowd instead, looking for something I hadn't seen a hundred times, looking for something that wouldn't add to the frustration building inside me. Something that would pull me out of my head for a while.

Like Aleena.

Immediately, I tried to shove the thought of her away, but she clung.

Thoughts of her clung.

Up on the stage, the domme was flogging her sub, but I felt like I was a million miles away, back in a restaurant, sitting with a wide-eyed girl from Iowa, listening as she talked about some of the silly things

48

that happened during what she probably considered a typical day.

All around me, people were engaged in all sorts of vice, some private, some not. A dozen feet away, there was a man with a women lying face down on his lap, her ass upturned as he brought down his hand in a rhythmic series of slaps. She moaned in a way that sounded a little too forced to be appealing.

Nothing here seemed to be appealing tonight.

My mind tried to wander back to the girl from earlier and in a bid to find something to distract myself, I focused back on the man and his chosen playmate for the night.

Her hair was dark and curling, not quite as lush and thick as Aleena's. Although her skin was a smooth warm tone, it looked more like the typical tanning bed gold than anything she'd been born with. Still...

I pictured myself in that very position and the woman who lay across my lap was Aleena.

My cock all but stood on end, blood draining straight down as that image coalesced. Her skin would be silken and smooth. She wouldn't have been spanked before, I already knew it. I'd start slow...

Somebody screamed and the fantasy fell apart.

But it didn't take much to bring it back to mind. I shifted my gaze to another couple, another threesome, to the woman being bound down below.

What would Aleena think? Would she be shock? Shamed? Aroused? Appalled?

Intrigued?

The sharp crack of a whip jerked my head around and I found myself staring at the stage, caught off-guard.

Well, maybe Mistress Rose did have something new in store.

She'd traded out the flogger for a whip and, just as she lifted her arm to bring it back down on his back a second time, he spoke.

A man—one of the few who lingered near the stage for just this purpose—lifted a hand.

A slight murmur of disappointment drifted through the crowd, but Mistress Rose immediately lowered her whip and rushed to the sub's side.

He'd spoken his safe word.

He was done.

I watched as they exited the stage and told myself to stop thinking about Aleena. Mistress Rose, I'd heard, was popular among the new subs. She enjoyed teaching them the ends and outs, and she loved the public aspects.

That wasn't for me.

This wasn't so much a *lifestyle* choice for me.

It was a need.

I craved the dark, driving edge that came with a woman's sexual submission. It let me lose myself, free myself. But I didn't have the patience, or the finesse, to teach anybody the ins and outs of this lifestyle. All my partners were people who knew what they liked and how far they wanted to go—and preferably, they preferred to go pretty damn far.

Aleena might not be completely innocent, but she was pretty close.

She deserved to stay that way.

Chapter 5

Aleena

I wasn't exactly unfamiliar with interviews, but when it came to this sort of thing, I was clueless.

The good news was that my wardrobe was basic. I don't mean minimalist, I mean non-existent. When you don't have that much to choose from, it made getting ready that much easier. My casual wear consisted of a few pairs of jeans and t-shirts. My work selection was a little more expansive, with three pairs of dress pants and white button blouses as well as a couple of dresses.

The dresses weren't appropriate for a job interview, or much of anything outside of holidays or the occasional wedding. Despite the cold, I went with the pants and short-sleeved shirt. Hopefully, the office building would be warm enough that I wasn't shivering through the entire interview.

Thanks to the two years of college courses I'd

taken, I knew I needed a résumé. I'd hit the internet, studying résumés and doing the best I could to make my pitiful work experience sound more impressive than it was.

Résumé and references in hand, I showed up and immediately felt lost.

Standing there in the lobby of a massive skyscraper, I realized I had no idea what company I was supposed to be looking for. With my résumé tucked inside a manila folder, I studied the company directory—it wasn't the kind I was used to seeing—it was digital and all flowery and pretty.

But it didn't help at all.

So I listened.

People talked.

All around me, conversation buzzed. Apparently, there was a *lot* of hiring going on today. I realized quickly that a single company owned the entire building.

Ooookay...

I started to work my way through the crowd, picking up scraps of conversation. Roughly one hundred positions available, everything from hospitality to housekeeping to secretarial.

At eight o'clock exactly, a man came into the lobby and the conversations ceased. I didn't know who he was, but he had the look of someone who expected people to do exactly what he said. Looking to be in his early forties, he had salt-and-pepper hair and dark blue eyes.

"My name is Robert Findlay and I'm the business manager for the Winter Corporation. I report directly to the CEO."

There was a faint murmur in the crowd and he smiled. "The CEO of the Winter Corporation takes a very hands-on approach, as some of you have probably heard." He paused a moment and smoothed down his tie. He had a matter-of-fact way about him and he spoke in such a manner that made you think he was talking personally, right to you. "There will be five interviews going on at the same time. The people you will be speaking with have a list of our available positions and will be determining which of you will be a good fit. If necessary, I may be called in to ask a few questions of my own. All decisions regarding hiring or second interviews for some of the more difficult positions will be made after all applicants have been seen. Calls will be made tomorrow morning."

I found myself nodding even though I barely registered anything he was saying.

My hands were sweaty on the folder I held in my hands and I struggled not to look around me. This was insane. Was there some sort of spot I should have put my name if I wanted to try to get in on the hospitality list? I hadn't seen any sort of sign-ups, but—

"Aleena Davison?"

Jerking my head, I found that Robson Findlay was looking around.

"What?"

He heard me and turned his head, smiling at me. "Aleena?"

Several eyes turned my way and, nervously, I smoothed a hand down my trousers than started toward him.

He nodded toward a door to the left. There was a woman standing there and she gestured me through. A few others followed and, without saying a word to anybody, I slid through.

About thirty minutes passed before I was called in to meet with a tall, thin man who gave me a friendly smile as I stood. I followed him back to an office cluttered with all sorts of television and movie memorabilia.

"My name's Frank," he said as he sat behind a desk. "I'm part of the HR department here at the Winter Corporation."

"It's nice to meet you," I said. I ran my hand over my lap as if I was smoothing down a skirt.

He held out his hand and I gave him my résumé. He took a moment to read it before looking back up at me. "From Iowa to the Big Apple? That's quite a move."

I nodded. "It's been a bit of an adjustment."

"I'll bet it has," he agreed. "Did you come with your family or a friend?"

"By myself," I said. I wondered if this was his way of trying to put me at ease, making small talk.

"And you didn't know anyone here?"

I shook my head.

"That's quite a brave step to make," Frank said. "Are you looking to be an actress, or musician?"

"Neither," I said. "Honestly, I don't know what I want to do with my life and New York seemed like a great place to find myself."

"I see here that, until recently, you worked in the food service industry." He moved away from my personal life onto professional. He tapped his finger on my résumé and glanced at me, brow lifted.

"Yes, sir," I said. I folded my hands on my lap, fighting the urge to fidget.

"And the reason for leaving?"

*And that will be all, ma'am...*I could hear the bell tolling now. "My employment was terminated," I said simply. I wasn't going to give excuses or blame anyone else. If he asked, I'd be honest, but I wasn't going to sit here and whine, either.

"Hmmm." Eyes narrowed, he leaned back in his seat and studied me. "Might I ask why?"

"I dropped some dishes," I said. I was tempted to add that I'd tripped, but I refrained.

"And you were fired for that?" He looked down at my résumé again. "If I called the restaurant, would they tell me the same story?"

"I don't know," I answered honestly again. "But if you request my time sheets, you'll see that I was never late or left early. As far as I know, I never had a customer file a complaint."

Frank looked at me, his eyes narrowing as they searched my face. I knew that look well enough to know that he was trying to determine if I was telling the truth. I didn't say a word or look away. I didn't have anything to hide.

When he returned his attention to my résumé, he moved on. "You have a degree in office management. Why didn't you try to get an office job?"

"I did," I answered. "But most of the businesses here want someone with at least a bachelor's degree or experience."

"But you have some experience," he pointed out.

"I worked for my dad," I said, smiling a little. "I was named one of the assistant managers in the restaurant my dad owns—I *earned* it, but I was only eighteen. It's probably not what people are looking for when they ask for experience."

He made a noise that could have meant anything. "Why didn't you choose to continue past your associate's degree?"

"Because I don't know if office management is what I want to do," I said. "I love the organizational part of it, the managing of schedules and making sure things run smoothly, but beyond that? I don't know if it's what I want."

"What *do* you want to do?" he asked, pushing at me.

"Honestly?" I looked away. "I don't know yet."

"You're a very straight-forward person, Ms. Davison." Frank leaned back in his chair.

"I've heard that once or twice."

"Will you excuse me for a moment?" he asked.

"Of course." He slipped outside, leaving me alone in his office. The TV memorabilia in there would have put some of the geek types into throes of geektastic orgasms.

I'd heard of some of the shows, but others, not so much. There were figurines and a lot of them were aliens, scattered among the odd spaceship. On one wall were pictures of groups of people, Frank included, dressed up and smiling. They were all done up in the sort of costumes I'd only seen online. One of the pictures even looked like it could've been from a costumed wedding.

The door opened again and I turned, ready to offer a polite compliment about his décor. Instead of Frank, however, a woman walked in. She looked like she was in her late thirties, but something about her dark eyes told me that her actual age was a few years older. She had dark hair with a few streaks of gray and the smile she gave me was friendly.

"Aleena Davison?" she asked as I stood.

"Yes, ma'am," I said, offering my hand.

"I'm Fawna Harris and I'll be continuing this interview."

"Oh." I hoped I hadn't done or said anything to Frank that had bothered him.

Either I was very transparent or she was a mind reader, because she gave me a faint smile. "I'm just making a few more specific inquiries, that's all." She gestured towards the chair again. "Please, have a seat."

I sat, still not completely reassured.

"Tell me a bit about yourself, Ms. Davison," Fawna said.

I did, skimming over the past few years and what had led me to New York.

"What do you think are your greatest strengths?"

I managed to smile, even though mentally, I wanted to groan. I *hate* this question.

"I'm organized, punctual and a bit of a perfectionist," I said. "Based on performance reviews at my job back in Iowa, I'm a hard worker."

"Those are all great job skills to list," Fawna said. "But what about you? Personally. What are your greatest strengths as a person?"

"Ahhh...well, I'm honest." I shrugged. As nerves jangled inside me, I smoothed a nonexistent wrinkle out of my pants. "I try not to be rude about it and I know when not to say anything, but I don't believe in sugarcoating things when the truth is just easier. Some people might see that as a weakness, but I think it's a strength."

As Fawna made a motion to continue, I straightened, feeling more confident.

"I already told Frank that I'm organized and I've mentioned that I'm punctual—those aren't business traits—those are *me* traits. My life is just easier if I stay organized and I don't like running behind. It throws me off balance, although I also know how to shift and go with the flow. Sometimes you have to make adjustments. I've got thick skin and I know how to tolerate people—sometimes you deal with some unpleasant types when you work with the public."

At that, Fawna laughed. "Only sometimes."

"Usually only once or twice a day," I replied with a straight face.

"And clearly, you have a sense of humor." Now she smiled at me.

"It helps with most things."

"Doesn't it?" She nodded, her expression revealing nothing. "And your weaknesses?"

61

I gave myself a moment to think. I could listen a dozen things—or more. But how many were *real* and how many were imagined? I just didn't know.

"I'm still learning how to speak up for myself. That can be a weakness, but I'm getting better at it," I said finally. "I put people ahead of myself, which can be a strength, but I sometimes take it too far, giving up something I want for reasons that most people would ignore. I don't have a lot of experience outside of working in restaurants—"

"You get experience by working," Fawna said, interrupting. She waved her hand as though this was the least of her concerns.

I managed a weak smile. "Well, I think that's about it." I hesitated and then added, "Although I'm not from here. I grew up in the Midwest. A lot of people seem to think that's an issue here."

"We don't." Fawna gave me that same easy smile. "Did you have a specific job in mind when you arrived?"

"No," I said.

"One final question, Ms. Davison. How did you hear about the open interviews today?"

Shit. Dominic hadn't said I shouldn't tell anyone that he'd given me the information, but the fact that Fawna asked told me that something about me being here had piqued her curiosity. I supposed this was one of those times that being truthful was going to be a weakness, but I wasn't going to lie. For all I knew, they hadn't advertised and saying that would get me kicked out.

"A man named Dominic Snow told me about the open interviews," I said. I thought I saw surprise flicker across her eyes, but then it was gone, if it had been there at all. "He didn't mention that it'd be a problem for me to just come in."

"It's not," Fawna said. She stood. "It was a pleasure to meet you, Ms. Davison. You'll receive a call from us tomorrow regarding our decision."

Well.

Okay, then.

***

Later that night, I had plans with Chinese food, beer and Molly.

It was the ideal way to get my mind off everything and it was even better since Emma wasn't home.

If I was lucky, she'd stay out late—or maybe just spend the night with her boyfriend.

With one eye on the clock, I jumped in the shower and hurried through it, scouring off a day of walking around New York City. I'd hit what felt like a hundred other places, including one of the second interviews. I thought I just might get that one, which was good. I didn't think anything was going to come of that interview at the Winter Corporation.

I was still dripping water when Molly knocked.

With a towel wrapped around me, I hurried to the door and checked the peephole. It was indeed her. I undid the series of locks and let her in. "Come on," I said, staying behind the door as she came inside and then shutting it immediately behind her.

As she playfully leered at me, I darted back into the bathroom and finished drying off.

"Where's the dragon?" she called through the door.

"Out. She wasn't here when I got in." I rubbed some lotion on and dragged on clothes before heading out with some cream and a towel for my hair. That was never a quick job and I needed it to be dry before I went to bed, even if that was a couple of hours from now.

Molly had the food set up on the coffee table and a case of beer sitting next to it.

"That looks perfect," I said, rubbing at my hair with a towel. I hadn't realized how much I needed to relax until now.

I plopped down next to Molly on the couch. The springs gave an overload squeak under my weight and I automatically shifted to find the spot that wouldn't jab into my ass. The couch had been here when I'd answered Emma's ad for a roommate and it had been here when *she* had moved in. No telling how old the thing was.

"How goes the job search?" Molly asked, passing me a can of beer.

It was frosty. The Chinese was hot. Maybe one night this week wouldn't totally suck.

"So-so." I shrugged as I cracked the top of the beer and took a drink. I wasn't huge on the taste, but tonight, it didn't matter. "I had a second interview at one place and it sounds promising. Then there was an open interview at the Winter Corporation."

"What's that?" Molly asked as she pulled her feet up underneath her. "Never heard of it."

"Me either," I admitted. "Guess they own hotels and airlines or something like that."

"So they're interviewing for pilots?" Molly grinned. "You holding out on me, Aleena?"

I broke open the take-out box and breathed in the scent of Kung Pao chicken. My favorite. "You're a real comedienne, Mol. Seriously. Why you wasting time serving tables anyway? You ought to be headlining somewhere."

"Here every day at six," she said, nodding soberly. Then she saluted me with her chopsticks.

As the two of us ate, I told her about my weird interview and how I'd found out about it to begin with. True to form, she was more interested in hearing about Dominic Snow than my job possibilities. I was willing to oblige, preferring to ogle him in memory as opposed to worrying about how I would make ends meet.

Before I knew it, it was nearing midnight and we'd drank our way through most of a twelve-pack. I'd also forgotten all about the weird day I'd had or the shit that had come before it. It was just another night, hanging out with Molly and talking about whatever happened to come to mind.

We were in the middle of a discussion about the most appropriate way for Gary to meet a painful death when the door opened and Emma came in. She stopped halfway into the room and looked around, taking in the cans and boxes we had scattered all around us. The expression on her face was more than eloquent.

"I'll clean it up," I said, holding a hand over my chest. "I promise."

I could all but see the steam coming out of her ears.

"Well, I guess this is one way to deal with your shitty life." Emma's snide comment didn't annoy me as much as it would have if I'd been sober.

Molly laughed, the loud raucous laugh of someone who was pretty well plastered. "*Her* shitty life? Why don't you take a look in the mirror? Nah, I know what it is. You want everyone to be as fucking miserable as you are." Molly stood up and she had to balance herself on the arm of the couch before she could take a step forward. With a snide grin in place, she pointed at Emma. "I get it. Really. You're a miserable bitch whose life has gone down the toilet—but that doesn't mean everyone else around you has to be that way too."

I opened my mouth to tell Molly to lay off, but by the time my beer-soaked brain got the message, Emma had already stalked off towards her bedroom.

I looked at Molly and she shrugged.

"That was harsh," I said.

"That was truth," Molly pointed out.

"That doesn't mean you need to say it," I said, shaking my head. But I didn't go after Emma.

I felt bad for her. Really. It had to be hard, coming to New York with a specific dream and never reaching it.

But Emma was so negative, about everything. Nothing was ever good enough and nobody ever did anything to her satisfaction.

You are late on the rent, a small voice pointed out. Guilt twisted in me. Yeah. There was that. She had a reason to be aggravated with me.

If I could get one of these jobs, I could get caught up on the money I owed her.

I really wanted something where I could make enough money and get my own place, but unless I was pulling in at least four grand a month, that wasn't likely. Rent in New York City was obscene. This small place cost almost fourteen hundred a month.

Finding an affordable place while I worked as a server was slim to none. My good mood gone, I drained the rest of my beer and reached for the last can.

My life had gone from not that great to lousy in the blink of an eye. What was worse, I had no idea what to do about it.

This sucked.

Chapter 6

Aleena

The sound of the band Journey came blaring out of my phone. A few days ago, determined to boost my self-confidence, I'd programmed the song, "Don't Stop Believing," as my default ring tone, telling myself it would help rev up my moral. Who knows, the positive thinking might help when potential employers called.

Right now, the song made me want to gouge out my eyes—and plug my ears.

A shard of pain went straight through my temples and I slapped out a hand, thinking of nothing but the desire to silence the phone.

I was halfway through the motion of throwing it when I realized it might be someone calling about an interview.

Groaning, I stabbed at the button to answer.

"Hello?" My mouth felt like it was full of cotton balls and shit. Maybe cotton balls made of shit.

"May I speak to Aleena Davison, please?"

"This is she." I sat up and rubbed at sleep-heavy eyes. Why had I drank so much last night?

"Good morning, Ms. Davison. This is Fawna Harris from the Winter Corporation."

Shock propelled me upright, and I immediately

wished I'd moved a little slower. The room swam around me and my stomach echoed the movement, nausea churning through me. I might not be ready to bow before the porcelain throne, but I wasn't terribly far off.

"We'd like you to come in today for a second interview with the CEO."

Shit. I so did not want to leave my bed today. But I needed the job.

Still... "Ah, an interview with the CEO?"

Had I understood that right?

"Yes." I thought I heard a smile in the other woman's voice. "For the position we have in mind, you might have a great deal of contact with him, so we need to make sure it's a match, professionally speaking."

I'd fallen into the twilight zone. There was no other explanation. "Don't take this the wrong way, ma'am, but you *did* mean to call Aleena Davison, correct? I'm twenty-one, most of my experience is in the food service industry? We met briefly yesterday?"

Fawna chuckled. "Yes, Ms. Davison...may I call you Aleena?"

"Yes. Please do." This was getting very weird.

"Very well, Aleena. Yes, I know precisely who I'm speaking to. Are you available to come in today?"

"Absolutely." I checked the time on the clock hanging across the room. I needed at least forty-five minutes to be presentable and then another forty-five minutes to get to Manhattan.

"Excellent. I see that this number is listed as your mobile contact, so I'll text you the address," Fawna said. "Can you be there by eleven?"

"Yes."

She said something else and I must have made the appropriate noise. She hung up and I sat there, staring dumbly at my phone. "That did not just happen."

"I hope to hell that was a job interview."

I looked up and saw Emma leaning against the counter of what could laughingly be called a kitchen. She held a cup of coffee. I would have sold my kidney to have a cup just then. "Excuse me?" I asked sourly.

"A *job* interview," she said, speaking slowly, as if I was an idiot.

"Yes." I tossed my phone down and got up off the sofa bed where I slept. I made a half-hearted attempt to straighten the bed while the pounding in my head increased. I was almost ready to puke by the time I had the frame tucked inside the sofa and the cushions back in place. Dismally, I looked at the small, cramped apartment. This was so not what I'd foreseen for my life here.

"Where?"

I frowned at Emma. "Where what?"

"Your interview," she said, tapping one finger on the coffee cup she held. Then she snorted. "Probably some two-bit diner where you'll pull in lousy tips. I'm not kidding, Aleena. You need to get your rent paid. You signed a contract, remember?"

"I know." Unwilling to waste any more time arguing with her, I turned away and moved toward the small cabinet where I kept my things. I needed some ibuprofen and a hit of caffeine and then I could deal with the rest of the day.

***

I had only one dress that might possibly work.

Simple and black, it was a faux-wrap dress I'd picked up off the clearance rack at Target back home. Although it looked good on me, I had a feeling I'd stick out like a sore thumb in the elegant offices of the Winter Corporation.

It had taken me a few weeks to get the hang of the subway system, but I was comfortable with it now. Well, mostly comfortable. I still didn't know how to handle the whistles, the catcalls or the ruder crap.

You'd be a lot prettier if you smiled, sweetie.

Damn...come on, honey, why don't you talk to me?

Don't be so stand-offish, bitch.

It was the same sort of garbage women put up with all the time. I'd learned how to deal with it by watching how others handled it, but even though I ignored them, it didn't make it any easier to tolerate.

Emerging from the subway, I blinked at the brilliance of the sunshine. My headache had retreated to tolerable levels and I'd chugged some tomato juice—a friend back home had always sworn by it. Something about the salt and the electrolytes and how alcohol robbed your body of those things, but tomato juice helped restore it.

I didn't feel normal, but I was a little steadier than I had been.

I had to walk a few blocks to get to the address I'd been given and that walk gave me a few minutes to clear my head and look around. I was so out of my league. People who lived around here didn't live paycheck to paycheck. They didn't even *look* at their paycheck. They would have accountants, I imagined, people who juggled the numbers and invested and advised.

They wore silk, Chanel and Dolce and Gabbana. They didn't wear clearance specials from Target.

Wrapping my coat more tightly around myself, I checked the discreetly marked houses. They all spoke of old money.

A woman strode down the sideway and caught sight of me then sniffed. As though I'd somehow changed the way the air smelled.

I didn't belong here.

Fake it until you make it, I told myself. I'd been doing that most of my life. Shoulders back, I gave her a brilliant smile and then turned up the next sidewalk.

The doorman smiled at me. "May I help you?"

"Hello, I'm Aleena Davison."

His eyes brightened. "Ms. Davison, you're expected." He opened the door and gestured for me to enter.

"Thank you," I said as I passed. My stomach was in knots. As I slid into the elevator, I pressed one palm against it. Nerves and a hangover are not a good mix.

"Floor, madam?" I jerked in surprise and then looked up. A uniformed man smiled at me.

"Ah...penthouse?"

He gave a polite nod and pushed a button.

Where was I? A place with guys whose only job was to punch buttons on an elevator all day?

Wonderland?

When I arrived at the top floor, the doors opened and I stepped out into a small lobby. There was only one door. My heart lurched as I moved toward it. Taking a deep breath, I stepped forward and knocked.

"Coming!"

I frowned at the sound of the man's voice, muffled by the door. Why did it sound familiar? As the doorknob turned, I fixed a professional expression on my face, just in time...

Holy shit. Just in time to see Dominic, standing there. He wore nothing but a towel.

Wow...heavy shoulders, sculptured chest, flat belly...and for the first time ever, I could understand why they called it a happy trail. I managed not to lick my lips, but it was a close call. *Interview, girl. You are here for an interview.*

And what in the world was Dominic Snow doing at the door?

"Dominic," I said.

"Aleena," he said. To say he looked puzzled was an understatement.

Glad to know I wasn't the only one.

"How did you know where I lived?"

Had I come to the wrong place? What were the odds?

Of course, if my brain hadn't been slightly alcohol-logged, maybe I would have been quicker on the uptake. Dominic Snow. The Winter Corporation. Clever. Dominic was the frickin' *CEO*—I'd bet my ass on it.

He took a step towards me and it took all my willpower not to put some distance between us. He smelled far too good, but if I moved, it'd be an admission.

"What are you doing here?" he asked, a faint smile kicking up the corners of his mouth. "And, don't take this wrong, but how did you find me?"

Self-preservation made me take a step back. "I'm here for a job interview."

The frown returned to his face. "I don't understand."

"I was told to come here for a second interview with the CEO of the Winter Corporation." I forced myself to keep my eyes on his face. I also told myself I wasn't at all curious about what lie under that towel. I was a big fat liar.

"An interview with me?"

"Which you would have known about had you answered your phone this morning." A woman's voice came from somewhere inside the vast space behind Dominic.

Dominic and I followed the sound of the voice.

I recognized Fawna right away. She stood framed in the wide, arched doorway of what looked to be a gorgeous kitchen. She nodded at me and then said, "Dominic, let the young lady inside, please."

He rolled his eyes and stepped aside, waving me in. Then he glanced at Fawna. "I would've answered my phone if you would've called." Dominic shut the door as he spoke.

Fawna held up a phone. "And you would've heard my call if you'd remembered to turn on your ringer."

Dominic winced, but it faded quickly, replaced by an engaging grin. "Aleena Davison, meet Fawna Harris, my...what did we decide your official title was?"

"Babysitter?" Fawna folded her arms across her chest and turned to me. "I apologize for the miscommunication, Ms. Davison. If I'd known Dominic was going to be parading around half-naked, I would've tried to get here earlier."

"I..." I started to make the typical *Oh, it's fine, that's okay, I understand* prattle, but in the end, honestly won out. "I don't understand."

"The position I want to hire you for is mine," Fawna said. "I'm not part of the Winter Corporation. Not exactly. I work directly for Dominic. I run his personal life. Basically, I'm his personal assistant." She ignored the sound of protest Dominic made and I kept my eyes on her. "I also coordinate with the household managers both here and at his house in the Hamptons to keep things running smoothly, for both day to day events and the occasional party."

"Your job?" I hoped I sounded professionally confused rather than completely clueless about life in general.

"I need to retire soon." Her expression was tight and I didn't even consider asking for a reason. "And I need someone to take over who can handle him."

"I don't need to be handled." Dominic's tone was mild.

At the same time, I was stuck on the words '*handle* him'. Was it terribly wrong that I wanted to take over the job of *handling* him? Just not the way she most likely intended. A blush heated my face and I shifted my gaze between the two of them. Clearing my throat, I said, "I'm not entirely sure I'm the right person for this job."

"Ten minutes ago, I would probably have agreed with you," Dominic said. He still stood there wearing nothing more than a towel—and he didn't seem at all concerned by that fact, either. "But you didn't bat an eyelash when I opened the door. For the way you're acting, I might as well be dressed in a three piece suit—or in rags. You don't seem to care one way or the other."

Oh, I care. I lifted a brow. "Is there a point to this, Mr. Snow?"

"You called me Dominic just a few minutes ago," he said, eying me closely. Then he shrugged. "The point is...Fawna's job doesn't deal only with the business side of my life. Let's just say this isn't the first time she's walked in on me wearing a towel."

"What exactly are you saying?" I asked, struggling to keep my voice calm.

It was hard, though. Something close to hope beat to life inside me, but I kept it under control.

Dominic looked at Fawna. She smiled and then looked at me. "I liked you for this almost from the first, Aleena. If you're interested in the job, I think you'd be a good fit. There will be some...well, let's call it on the job training, but if you're as sharp as I think you are, you'll catch on fast. For...unexpected reasons, I'm retiring at the end of the month. That's three weeks from now. That can be your probationary period and I'll be on hand to train you and help out with any questions, although I'm only on hand six hours a day—Mondays, Wednesdays and Fridays." She paused and then asked softly, "Are you interested?"

I swallowed and reached up to touch the necklace I wore.

Dominic's gaze followed my fingers.

"Are you interested?" Dominic asked when I stayed quiet.

"Ah..."

"Dominic, why don't you go get dressed?" Fawna suggested softly.

He opened his mouth as though to argue and then sighed, pushing a hand through his still-damp hair.

As he left us alone, Fawna took my arm and guided me over to the low, plush couch. At that moment, it looked as long and as wide as a river. We sat and she reached for a folder that had been sitting on the table. "Here's the job description," she said. "I understand you've never worked as a personal assistant before, but you've already made it clear that you have broad interests and you're organized. Organization is the most important thing for this job. The second...well, as Dominic noted, you didn't just gape at him when he opened the door."

I licked my lips and slid her a quick glance. "Ever heard the phrase *fake it until you make it*?"

"I have." She pursed her lips as she studied me. "You faked it very well then."

She placed the job description in my hand and I looked down to read it over.

"As you can see, you'll help handle his day to day activities, dealing with his travel plans, his correspondence—and he gets a lot of it. Some of it will be confidential and you'll be required to sign a non-disclosure agreement." Her voice became firm and I glanced up at her. Once she was sure she had my attention, she continued. "If you disclose any of his personal information, Aleena, there will be consequences. I'm certain you're discreet, but it's very important you understand this."

"I understand," I said.

"Excellent." She nodded back to the sheet of paper. "His travel plans can sometimes be irksome—he'll schedule a trip, then change his mind, and then change it again. Parties...well, those are a nuisance, but once he lets you know what he has in mind and the venue, you'll contact the person who runs that chosen venue to handle the details. For instance, if it's here, the household manager is Ramirez. Ramirez would manage most of the details and he will be happy to guide you through anything he needs your help with."

"That..." I blew out a breath. "This doesn't sound too overwhelming."

"The first few weeks will be," she said bluntly. "Just be advised."

"The first weeks of any new job usually are." I managed a weak smile. Then I asked the question I'd been almost too afraid to ask. "What's the job pay?"

"It's salary." She named a figure that made my jaw drop. And it dropped even more when she said, "There is a raise every year based on performance, top of the line health coverage, a retirement package and, of course, living quarters."

"Ah...living..." I cleared my throat, unsure if I heard her right. "Living quarters?"

She smiled. "Yes. There's a suite on the second floor here at the penthouse."

I reached up and rubbed my forehead. I was

starting to feel like I'd fallen down a rabbit hole. "Okay...what's the *bad* news?"

"The hours," she said bluntly. "Dominic can be a demanding boss. You can expect to work from seven in the morning to roughly six in the evening, five days a week. He expects his assistant to be on call and willing to work as needed on weekends. With that said, your weekends, generally, are your own." She tucked her hair back and gave me a tired smile. "Currently, though, we're working a lot on the weekends. Dominic is in the midst of opening a new business and it's taking up a great deal of his time so he'll need more from you—actually *us*—until that's done. I told him I wanted to see this job through. We started it together, so I wanted to finish it together."

Numb, I looked back down at the job description she'd given me.

Organizing parties.

Handling correspondence.

Travel plans.

Communicating with the household staff.

Staring at Dominic when he walked around in a towel—okay, *that* qualified as a bonus.

"I'm a waitress," I said quietly. "I've got an associate's degree in business. The closest I've come to organizing a party was when the local Girl Scouts asked if they could have a fund raiser at our restaurant and my dad put me in charge."

"Oh?" Fawna smiled, seeming to be genuinely interested. "How did it go?"

"Pretty good." I shrugged. "But it was small change compared to...this."

"Do you need some time to think about it?" Fawna asked.

I took a deep breath. "No. Either I'm dreaming or I've just received the biggest break of my life."

Fawna chuckled. "In a few weeks, you might think it was the *worst* break. Now...here's the big question, because I know how things go when it comes to rental agreements in New York. How much notice do you need to give where you're staying?"

Chapter 7

Dominic

I didn't let myself look back as I jogged upstairs to change.

But I couldn't keep myself from looking down the hall toward Fawna's suite.

Fawna's suite was at the end of the hall. It wasn't very big, but it had its own bathroom, a small kitchenette and a small living room.

She hadn't been there or at the guest house in the Hamptons much lately, spending most of her time at the hospital. I'd gotten used to having her nearby. She was a friend—more than a friend, really.

Now somebody else would be living in those quarters.

Not just somebody.

Aleena.

Heat spread through me at the thought of having her so close by, but at the same time, there was also wariness. I don't know how I felt about having her work under me. I'd rather just have her *under* me.

Sure, I'd wanted her to get a job, but this job? No.

I dressed quickly, opting for comfort in jeans and a sweatshirt, since I wasn't leaving the penthouse today.

A soft laugh caught my attention and I glanced toward the stairs—and Aleena.

What had I been thinking?

Was I being an idiot?

Or was I thinking with my cock instead of my head?

Fawna had been an easy choice. We generally saw eye-to-eye on how things should be done and she didn't take bullshit from me—those were two very good reasons why she'd done so well as my assistant.

The third, and most important, reason, was that she'd always been there.

She'd been my English teacher when I was twelve and had found out that I was adopted. Through coincidence or fate, she'd been moved up a grade the following year and had been there for me when my parents divorced. She'd been the only one of my teachers to fight when I'd been expelled and the only one who'd checked in on me regularly.

She'd left teaching some years ago, but we'd stayed in touch. I'd reached out to her after I started my first company and offered her the job as my personal assistant.

She'd accepted and here she was, about to hand me off.

I headed back down the stairs, wondering if Aleena would still be there. She wasn't, but Fawna was waiting on the couch. I sat down in the chair across from her.

"I thought you were going to give me a list of names," I said. "Names that we'd go through together."

She gave me that amused smile that said, no matter how old or rich I got, she would always see the hyper-active boy who none of the other teachers wanted to deal with. "I arranged for a second interview."

"One that I didn't know about." Slumping in the seat, I stared at her.

She raised an eyebrow at me, staring until I had to concede the point. "All right, one that I would've known about if I'd paid attention."

"Should we call her back and tell her we need a third interview? Or perhaps more time...?" she gave me an out.

Instead of answering, I leaned forward. "Why her? Out of almost a hundred people, you picked her as a possible candidate for your job?"

"No," she said. "I picked her as the *only* candidate."

"Okay," I said. "That still doesn't tell me why."

"You told her about the interviews and put her name on the list."

I stood up and went to the kitchen. I needed something to eat. Fawna followed.

"Dominic, if you hadn't seen something in the girl in the first place, you wouldn't have made a point of putting her name on the list."

I sighed as I pulled out leftover pizza and put it on a plate. "It was my fault she got fired."

"How was it your fault?"

Aggravated, I explained, ending with a pointed explanation of just what I'd like to do to that dickless dickhead Aleena had worked for.

"It doesn't sound like it was anybody's fault that he fired her—save for his ego," Fawna said. She reached out and patted my cheek, keeping the contact light and quick. "Dominic, he was an ass. She had a mishap. It should have just been excused and forgotten about. It was kind that you tried to help."

She eyed my pizza with disgust. "You know, the entire point of you having a professional chef four days a week is so you can have options—nutritional, tasty options—to choose from the other three."

I grinned at her as I pushed the buttons on the microwave. "There's only so much casserole and pasta that a man can eat."

"I have a better idea—have him *teach* you to cook. That way, when you get bored with what he prepares you, you can start making your own food."

I started to argue with her.

Then she played her trump card. "It would horrify your mother."

"Huh." The microwave dinged and I opened it, the rich, spicy tang of pizza flooding the air. "You're right. It would."

"A boy your age should be able to fend for himself—and exist on something other than pizza."

Sending her a sidelong look, I said, "Nobody other than you calls me a *boy*, Fawna."

She gave me the look that had stopped me in my tracks back when I'd been in her sixth grade English class. I wasn't in sixth grade anymore. Yet it still worked.

"Back to Aleena." I tested the pizza. It was way too hot. That meant it was perfect. "She has a degree in office administration. I figured she'd get a spot as a secretary or maybe a desk clerk at one of the hotels."

"It's an associate's degree and she has no experience." She moved to the refrigerator and opened it, pulling out a pitcher of lemonade. She held it up with a questioning look. After I nodded, she pulled down two glasses. "She likely would do fine working at one of the hotels, but Frank had her for an interview, and he saw...well, likely the same thing I do, possibly the same thing you do. She's got spark, Dominic. She's got the kind of honesty and backbone one needs to handle you—"

At the thought of Aleena *handling* me, my brain immediately took a right turn into all the dark and dirty places I'd love to take her. All the dark and dirty places she would probably *never* go.

Unaware of my train of thought, Fawna offered me a glass of lemonade. I took it and gulped half of it down while she continued. "And she's smart. I think she can handle this job, Dominic. But if you have doubts..."

"You don't," I said gruffly. Putting down the lemonade, I grabbed the hunk of pizza from my plate and bit in. After I'd swallowed the bite, I said, "You hired her."

"You're the CEO. You hired her." She smiled at me.

She sipped at her lemonade. I finished up the first slice of pizza and devoured the second before either of us felt inclined to speak again.

"How's the little guy doing?"

"Eli is..." She took a deep, steadying breath. "He's doing well enough." Her expression softened.

"One more month. The doctors think he'll be strong enough to leave the hospital in another month."

I thought of the tiny little baby, struggling to live, a machine doing his breathing for him.

I reached over and caught Fawna's hand. "You know that you and Eli are both welcome to live here or at the house for as long as you need. Just say the word."

"I know," Fawna said, giving me a fond smile. "But I've found a place outside the city."

My hand tightened on hers while my throat clogged. I was losing a piece of myself and I knew it. I just didn't know what to do about it. Actually, that was the problem—I knew what to do about it— *nothing*.

She needed a new start, her and her little grandson.

The past year had sucked. She'd lost her daughter and she'd nearly lost her grandbaby.

Shortly after she'd started working for me, her daughter, Kelsey, had dropped out of college and moved in with her boyfriend. At some point in the years that followed, Kelsey had gotten mixed up in drugs and it had gotten progressively worse.

Nothing anybody did seemed to help.

Every time the phone had rung, Fawna had been sure it would be the police, saying they'd found Kelsey's body. Then, about six months ago, Kelsey had called. She was pregnant, and still using. She wanted to come home.

Fawna had brought her daughter home and for a short while, I'd thought, *hoped*, maybe it would work.

Kelsey had only been in her six month when she'd gone into labor. She'd been underweight and sick a great deal too. She'd starting bleeding shortly after delivery and they hadn't been able to save her. The baby had made it...barely. The poor little guy was now a month old, but he still had a long road ahead of him.

"Poor guy," I said, focusing on the baby instead of her leaving. "Spending the first two months of his life in the hospital."

"He's a tough little guy." Fawna squared her shoulders. "He's going to be fine."

"Of course he is." I hugged her. "He takes after his grandma."

She laughed, but the sound was tired. "Grandma," she repeated, shaking her head. "Sometimes, I still don't believe it."

After a moment, she moved away, taking her glass and sipping from it as she stared out the window. My penthouse faced out over Central Park and she gazed at the view as if she didn't see it. "You asked me why I chose Aleena," she said as she turned back towards me. "I picked her because I think she's exactly what you need."

I stared at her for a moment, unsure how to respond to such a statement. Before I could come up with anything, however, my phone rang. Fawna glanced at it and her face hardened.

Shit. I knew what that meant.

"You should get that, and I should get going." She turned away. "I'm going to arrange to have what I won't need for the next few weeks put in storage."

I'd arranged for her to stay in a suite of rooms close to Eli's hospital. Lately, she wasn't here very often; it shouldn't be such a shock to think about her putting her things in storage, to think about her leaving.

But it was.

As the phone rang again, I looked down.

As Fawna slid out, I answered it. "Hi, Mom."

"Darling. It's not a bad time, I hope?"

I grimaced and lied. "No, Mom. I'm working from home today."

"That's nice."

Those words were followed by a stilted silence. I didn't bother to try and fill it. We'd never handled small-talk well.

"How's Fawna's grandson doing?"

I scowled at the phone. "He's improving. The doctors think he'll be able to leave within the next month."

"Such a long time," my mother said quietly.

"Yeah."

Another pause.

Fawna and my mother had never gotten along well, mostly because of my mother. Fawna had tried, more than once, to reach out. I think some part of my mother was jealous, envious of the easy relationship I shared with Fawna. They'd practically adopted me, raised me...and I connected better with a teacher I saw for a few minutes a day than I did with my parents.

Of course, that teacher had *tried*.

She'd reached out.

She'd made it seem like I mattered, that I was more than my pedigree.

My parents loved me, and I knew that, but they didn't know how to handle children. Most of my childhood, I'd been raised by nannies, trotted out on holidays and special occasions. Other than that, I was off to one boarding school or another. Eventually, I'd had my fill of them and rebelled, getting in trouble. It wasn't long before I'd been brought home. The local private schools hadn't been much better and listening to my parents fight definitely hadn't helped.

I probably would have turned out okay, if it wasn't for—

Don't. I jerked my thoughts to a halt before they

could go down that dark, ugly path. *Don't go there.*

"I spoke to Fawna yesterday. I hadn't heard from you for a few days and I...well, I called her to see how everything was. She said you were busy looking for her replacement...?"

She left the question open-ended. Reaching up to pinch the bridge of my nose, I tried to ignore the headache that was building. "I'm hiring a new PA, yes, but there's no replacing Fawna. She's one of a kind."

I didn't bother to ask why she hadn't called me. Instead, I repeated, "There's no replacing Fawna."

"Yes, you've always been...fond of her," she said, her voice growing tight. My mother still believed I loved Fawna more than her.

That wasn't true—entirely. I did love my parents, although there was no denying that Fawna understood me better. She'd always been there, even when my parents weren't, when they couldn't be. My mother had believed that Fawna and I were lovers, an idea that personally leaves me really disturbed, since I see Fawna as a mother-figure, of sorts.

Not that I'd tell my own mother that. I've got enough parental issues as is. I don't need to add to them.

"Other than being busy, everything is well?" she asked, her voice taking on an edge.

I sighed and closed my eyes. Over a decade and

we still couldn't have a normal mother-son conversation. "Yes, Mom. I'm fine. Just busy. My new business is opening in a couple weeks and I have a lot to do for it."

"Right," she said. "The match-making company."

"Yep. My match-making company. My little project."

"Did you need any help with it? Connections? Money?"

"It's all good, Mom." I didn't remind her that my net worth was now twice what hers and my father's had been when they'd been married. She'd helped finance my first hotel purchase, but I'd paid her back with interest less than two years later.

"Beatrice Rittenour was saying that her daughter, Penelope, was talking about signing up for your services. I'm sure you remember her."

It was a good thing my mother wasn't here to see my face. The sneer would have appalled her. Penelope...yeah, I remembered her. She was three or four years younger than me and had already been well-groomed to take her mother's place as the public face of the Rittenour fortune, complete with the plastic smile and ability to turn any compliment into an insult.

"Have you considered using your company to see what eligible women are out there for you?"

And now we were at the real reason for the call.

"Since you've expressed your desire for me to remain out of your romantic affairs, this might be a good way for you to see what your options are."

"Mom." I kept my voice polite, but firm. "That wouldn't be very professional of me." I didn't add that I didn't give a fuck if she thought the women I saw were 'appropriate' or not. It didn't even matter that I wasn't planning on settling down with anyone in the first place.

"Dominic, darling—"

"I'm not getting married, Mom," I snapped. "We've had this discussion before. It's not going to happen, and certainly not with someone like Penelope Rittenour. I've seen firsthand how those kinds of marriages end up."

"Your father and I—" she began.

"No," I interrupted again. "I'm not talking about this. You said you called to see if I was okay. Well, I am. I'm busy with work and helping Fawna take care of things with Eli. Was there something else you wanted?"

Silence.

I hated talking to her this way.

I hated this chasm between us.

But she refused to understand that the man she wanted me to be and the man I already was were a world apart.

97

The world she lived in and the world I wanted to live in couldn't be any more different.

Her world was benefits and banquets and society functions.

If I had my way, I'd lose myself in work from the time I woke up, right up until...oh...eight or nine o'clock, then I'd lose myself between the thighs of a woman. Then I'd sleep and start the cycle all over again. Making money was a game and sex was the release.

That was all my world needed to be.

Society could go fuck itself.

But that concept was foreign to my mother.

"I'm sorry, Dominic. I'm just..." She paused and when she spoke again, her voice was quieter. "I just worry about you. I'm sorry to bother you."

She hung up and I was left feeling guilty. I don't know if that was her intent, but it left me wanting to throw the phone. Instead, I put it down with controlled force and turned, bracing my hands on the counter as I stared ahead at the cabinets.

I saw absolutely nothing.

My relationship with my mother still felt completely broken.

I guess I should give her some credit. At least she *tried*. That was more than my father had done. We hadn't spoken in a decade and change. Ever since—

Dark, ugly blasts of memory swamped me and I shoved away from the counter. Driving the heels of my hands against my eyes, I tried to blot out those memories, but they never stayed buried for long. I could lose myself in work or I could lose myself in booze or I could lose myself in vice. If I didn't stay busy, though, the ghosts of my past found me.

I'd decided a long time ago, I wasn't going to end up drowning in alcohol, so I did the logical thing. I left the kitchen and headed for my home office.

I had work to do.

I wondered if Aleena had any idea what she'd gotten herself into.

Chapter 8

Aleena

Emma had taken the check—and my news—with surprising good grace.

My rental agreement with her did indeed have a provision for what happened if I moved out without giving her sufficient notice. It was kind of necessary, and I got why. She'd be up a creek without a paddle if she constantly had roommates not holding up their financial end of the bargain and yeah, I was one who had been slacking.

I'd been surprised with a sign-on bonus, and Fawna, in an act of extraordinary kindness, had given it to me immediately, instead of waiting ninety days as was typical. "I'm sure you need to square things with your roommate," she'd told me. She had *no* idea how badly I needed to square things with my roommate. I'd paid Emma for this month's rent and an additional month, according to the rental agreement if I left without giving sufficient notice.

And—*bonus*—I still had money left to put in the bank for once. That meant I was able to do some shopping. I'd needed it, too, because my business wardrobe was woefully non-existent. Molly had come through in spades there, taking me to a dozen kitschy little consignment shops where I found barely worn designer suits and retro pieces that made me feel like a million dollars.

Now, three days later, Molly lay on the new bed in my new room and stared up at the skylight.

Dominic had tried to insist I allow him to pay for a moving service. I'd put my foot down, while Fawna had quietly laughed from the side. Molly and I had just finished bringing in the last of my stuff and I was thoroughly exhausted.

"This is so unreal," she said, sighing happily. Then she slid me a look. "And your boss....oh, my goodness. Want to talk about *unreal*...honey."

Dominic hadn't been happy about my refusal so he'd shown up at my door both yesterday and today. The sight of him hefting boxes was one that would linger with me for a long time to come. Muscles bulging under worn tees, jeans clinging to strong thighs...

Stop drooling over your boss. I managed a casual smile for Molly. "Yeah, tell me about it. You should see him in just a towel."

Molly laughed while I rubbed at my stiff neck.

I dropped down on the scoop-styled chair that had come with the apartment. Both Fawna and Dominic had told me I could have the place redecorated however I wanted, but I like how it looked. It was bright, airy, and feminine without being fussy. And *mine*...I hadn't ever dared hoped for someplace like this. Not even once. Well, not after I saw what New York real estate went for.

"How did Emma take the news?" Molly asked, bonelessly shifting position and rolling onto to her belly.

"Well, once I ponied up the money for the rent for this month and next?" I shrugged. "She couldn't have cared less." Then, wrinkling my nose at her, I added, "But you should have seen the look on her face when I told her about my new job. You would have thought she'd swallowed a whole lemon."

"I bet." Molly hooted with laughter. "You found the golden goose, baby. I mean...wow. I knew the guy looked familiar, but I had no idea that *Dominic Snow* was one of *the* Snows."

I drew up my knee, instinctively glancing toward the door. Dominic wasn't here. He'd left after we'd finished bringing up the boxes. While he was gone, I planned to unpack what precious little I owned and settle in.

Molly had a shift starting in less than three

hours and once she left…

I swallowed the knot that formed in my throat.

Once she left, I'd be on my own in a world that felt so alien.

It was Saturday, my first official day of living here. Monday, I'd started my new job, although I'd been going through the motions for the past two days with Fawna walking me through things while I took a hundred thousand notes.

"I'm gonna have to go soon, girl," Molly said with a sigh, moving into a sitting position. She stared at me. "What are you going to do?"

"Take a bath." I grinned at her. "I've been dying to try that tub out."

"Hmmm." Molly waggled her brows at me. "Maybe I could stay a little longer. We can make it a double."

"Pervert." I made a face at her. Molly flirted with just about anything with a pulse and I was used to it by now. Throwing one of the decorative pillows at her, I picked up the folder lying on the table next to the chair. "I've got homework for later. Fawna left me with all of this to go over. At some point, she tells me I'll have all of this memorized."

I eyed it dismally, wondering just how it was possible.

Molly rose and came toward me. "What is it?"

Protectively, I covered it with my hand. "Sorry.

Private." I shrugged. "A lot of the stuff I do for him falls under '*If I tell you, I have to kill you*' territory, I think."

"Man, he's James Bond...I *knew* it."

"Exactly." I rolled my eyes and put the folder down, tucking it into the space between my seat and the table, out of sight. "If you're heading out, I'll walk you to the elevator. I want to grab some lunch anyway."

"Okay. Speaking of lunch...we need to make plans to meet. You're all the way across town now." Molly's face took on a glum cast.

Impulsively, I hugged her. "I know. We'll make plans for next week, maybe?"

"I'm working Saturday. Sunday?"

"Done." We headed toward the elevator, talking although my mind was already on that bath.

***

After Molly left, I slipped back inside and pressed my back to the door, staring at the world I'd somehow tumbled into.

"Welcome to Wonderland, Alice."

Although the bath in my suite called me, I hadn't had a chance to explore, not really. Licking my lips, I chanced a glance back at the door.

Dominic was still gone.

Slowly, I moved around the open area that was both living room and dining room. The dining table was set up in front of a broad, floor to ceiling window that stared out over Central Park. I stood there a moment, staring down over the green. It only intensified my feeling that I was no longer in any sort of world I recognized.

It wasn't entirely a comfortable feeling, so I moved away, hurrying into the kitchen. This place, at least, was one where I knew what I was doing. I'd always liked to cook and both Fawna and Dominic had assured me I was welcome to use the area as often as I wanted. There was a professional chef who came in for Dominic, and I was told he'd be available for me as well, but I couldn't imagine anybody cooking for me.

It had been forever since I'd been able to really *cook*. That miniscule kitchen back at Emma's place barely qualified as a real kitchen and I couldn't make anything without crashing into one counter or the other. There was no way to make a real meal without stopping half way through to wash the pots and pans.

Leaving the gleaming surfaces and polished chrome, I padded down the hallway to find the offices where I'd be working with Dominic when we stayed in. More windows, letting light pour in. I saw a desk that I assumed was mine and a massive one that could only be his.

It was also in a state of semi-organized chaos. I grimaced. Fawna had told me on Friday why she was leaving and my heart broke for her. It also explained why the office was in this state. The meticulous woman wouldn't allow this, but she had other priorities now.

As I continued through the penthouse, I found two more bedrooms with their own bathrooms. One of the beds struck me as unusual, although I couldn't figure out why.

The last two rooms downstairs were a pantry and laundry room.

If you had replicated—no, triplicated—the apartment I'd shared with Emma, you could have fit the entire thing into the downstairs alone and had room left over.

Upstairs, the only rooms were mine and Dominic's. My personal apartment, complete with its own personal kitchenette, a sitting room, a bathroom and its own laundry was double the size of my old place. But Dominic's rooms dwarfed it. I paused in the open doorway for just a minute, just long enough to bring in his scent, so that it flooded my head.

It was slightly spicy and wholly male, the very same scent that had surrounded me the day we'd met. It was the same cologne he'd been wearing that fateful day.

"Stop it," I told myself, pushing away from the door.

But the memory followed me, all the way into my rooms. Closing the door behind me, I then leaned against it. My nipples peaked and stiffened against my bra.

I thought of his arms, bare and glistening from his shower.

What would it be like, I wondered, to have those arms around me? To lick away the droplets of water that had rolled down his chest?

Frustration burned inside me and I shoved away from the door, striding into the bathroom. As I walked, I jerked off my shirt, tossing in the general direction of the wicker basket that Fawna had left behind. I dumped my shoes in the closet, and then I tossed my yoga pants and underwear toward the basket as well.

If I was going to daydream about my boss, I might as well get it over with—and make the most of it.

The tub filled fast and the water was hot. I eased myself down and fiddled with the controls until the jets pulsed around me and then I gave into the urge.

I could still picture those drops of water, running down his chest. My hands flexed, itching to follow the path of those droplets, and my mouth went dry, aching to follow the trail of one droplet in particular. The one that rolled down the slope of his pectoral and clung to his left nipple for what seemed like an eternity.

My peripheral vision had always been excellent.

Now, as I remembered, my own nipples tightened and I shivered as the water lapped at my skin. I slid a hand down my belly and imagined it was his. His hands had been hard, and just the slightest bit rough. To feel them on me...

I whimpered as I parted my flesh and started to stroke myself.

Heat spread across my skin as his hands caressed me. I could almost feel it.

This isn't smart.

But the throbbing between my legs didn't care about smart and the arousal driving me was stronger than anything I'd felt in a long time, maybe ever. Fuck being smart.

I cupped my breast with my free hand, rolling my nipple, as I imagined that it was Dominic, his touch strong and certain, just the slightest bit rough. Not too rough, though, and never with the intent to hurt.

I moaned as I imagined his teeth scraping across my neck, then down to my nipples before he moved lower, and lower...

My fingers stroked through the wet curls, the water pulsing and pounding all around me. *Dominic's hand*, I thought, circling my clit.

Arousal jolted through me.

I whimpered as my mind fed me an image of him going to his knees before me, that golden blond head between my thighs, his mouth worshipping me. His tongue—what would that be like? I wouldn't know, of course. Nobody had ever gone down on me before.

A moan tore out of me as I pushed two fingers inside my pussy. I imagined it was Dominic and my muscles spasmed around my fingers. At the same time, I arched up. The heel of my hand pressed against my clit and the pressure sent delight arcing through me.

Images flashed through my mind.

Dominic's ass flexing as he rode me.

The way he would feel inside me, stretching me.

Those eyes, those bright blue eyes watching me as our bodies came together over and over again.

The pressure building inside me exploded and I came with a muffled cry. My blood roared in my ears, my heart thudded fast and hard.

I was about ready to release a long sigh of completion when everything in me froze.

"Ms. Davison?"

Shit!

Dominic...

I slammed my hand against the panels of the tub. "Yes?" It came out more a squeak than anything else.

"I've got Thai out here if you're hungry..." There was a pause. He was in my room.

"Ah. Okay. I'm um...I need a few minutes, Mr. Snow. I'll meet you downstairs!"

Chapter 9

Dominic

With spring rolls and curry spread out in front of me, I called myself ten kinds of idiot.

But I wasn't sure why.

Because I'd gone to get food for us instead of out to Olympus liked I'd planned?

Or because I'd dumped the food and followed the sound of the throaty moans I'd heard coming from the bathroom?

My cock was so hard now, so ready, I could feel the drops of pre-come leaking from it. But had I gone into that bathroom and knelt beside the tub? Had I taken her mouth in mine, slid my hand below the water to see what she was doing to make her moan so sweetly?

No.

I was scooping out rice and listening for the sound of her footsteps.

This was a mistake, I told myself.

113

It wasn't the first time and I doubted it would be the last.

She was quiet.

Fawna hadn't been that quiet.

It took me off guard to look up and find her standing in the door, wearing a faded pair of jeans and a worn T-shirt with a blue fish and the words *Just Keep Swimming*. She hovered there, looking flustered and so damn beautiful. All I wanted to do was back her up against the wall and strip her naked, then take up where she had left off.

Instead, I nodded to the food.

"Are you hungry?"

She nodded. "Yeah." She nibbled on her lower lip as she came in. "I...uh...is there anything you need me to do for you?"

Yes. Tell me what you were doing in the bathtub and then let me do it all over again.

I gave her a tight smile. "No. You don't officially start until Monday, Ms. Davison. Now...help yourself."

As she came closer, I turned away.

I needed to get my head examined.

How had I possibly thought this could work out?

***

114

"Tell me what will please you, master."

The sub was beautiful. Her red hair was short, cut close to her skull like a sleek, silken cap. Her skin was pale as moonlight and her eyes were blue as the summer sky. She was lush and soft, her curves ripe and she'd fill my hands to perfection.

In short, she was as different from Aleena as she could be.

I didn't imagine it would make much difference, but maybe I could avoid calling her the wrong name.

I gestured to the floor and she knelt.

Reaching up, I cupped one breast in my hand, rolling the nipple until it peaked. She rubbed her cheek against my thigh, close to my cock. Deliberately, I closed my eyes and thought of Aleena.

"Take my cock out," I said.

She did and I imagined it was another woman's hands on me.

When she started to stroke me, I opened my eyes. "Did I tell you to do that?"

She froze, but it wasn't fear in her eyes. It was excitement.

"Stand up."

When she did, I bent her over the table. Need drove me, although it wasn't need for her. It didn't matter. She was all that was available—well, not all. I

115

could have had any number of women here, but the woman I wanted wasn't here.

Bringing my hand down on her ass, I listened as she gasped. It was nothing like the broken little moan I'd heard coming from Aleena's bathroom.

"Don't make a noise," I told her.

The second time I spanked her, she bit back the sound. She swallowed her moan the third time and it was closer... "That's it," I muttered.

Nudging her thighs apart, I pulled out a rubber.

A few eyes came our way, but I ignored them. Public sex wasn't normally my game, but if I stopped now, I might slip out of my head again and I needed the release.

I spanked the sub again and she made the same, low husky noise. I drove in, gripping her hips hard. "Don't come," I ordered her. I fucked her fast, hard, feeling my orgasm racing closer, picturing another woman bent over me, another woman struggling to hold back her climax.

Aleena—

"Please, master, let me come!" she begged.

I brought my hand down hard on her ass and she cried out, climaxing around me with brutal intensity. The internal milking of her pussy around my cock brought on my own release.

And in my mind, it was Aleena.

Come for me, Aleena...come...

As I came down from the intense orgasm my thoughts drifted. Tomorrow is Monday; the day Aleena officially starts working as my personal assistant. How will I ever be able to control myself, not rip her clothes off, bend her over and fuck her right in the office? I couldn't help but smile at the thought.

Continues in Serving HIM Vol. 2, release May 25th.

Acknowledgement

First, we would like to thank all of our readers. Without you, our books would not exist. We truly appreciate each and every one of you.

A big "thanks" goes out to all the Facebook fans, street team, beta readers, and advanced reviewers. You are a HUGE part of the success of the series.

I have to thank our PA, Shannon Hunt. Without you our lives would be a complete and utter mess. Also a big thank you goes out to our editor Lynette and our wonderful cover designer, Sinisa. You make our ideas and writing look so good.

About The Authors

MS Parker

M. S. Parker is a USA Today Bestselling author and the author of the Erotic Romance series, Club Privè and Chasing Perfection.

Living in Southern California, she enjoys sitting by the pool with her laptop writing on her next spicy romance.

Growing up all she wanted to be was a dancer, actor or author. So far only the latter has come true but M. S. Parker hasn't retired her dancing shoes just yet. She is still waiting for the call for her to appear on Dancing With The Stars.

When M. S. isn't writing, she can usually be found reading– oops, scratch that! She is always writing.

Cassie Wild

Cassie Wild loves romance. Every since she was eight years old she's been reading every romance novel she could get her hands on, always dreaming of writing her own romance novels.

When MS Parker approached her about co-authoring the Serving HIM series, it didn't take Cassie many seconds to say a big yes!!

Serving HIM is only the beginning to the collaboration between MS Parker and Cassie Wild. Another series is already in the planning stages.

Made in the USA
Coppell, TX
11 April 2022